Lazy Daisy, Cranky Frankie

Mary Ellen Jordan & Andrew Weldon

www.av2books.com

Go to **www.av2books.com**, and enter this book's unique code.

BOOK CODE

Q137636

AV² by Weigl brings you media enhanced books that support active learning.

First Published by

ALBERT WHITMAN & COMPANY

Publishing children's books since 1919

AV² Readalong Navigation

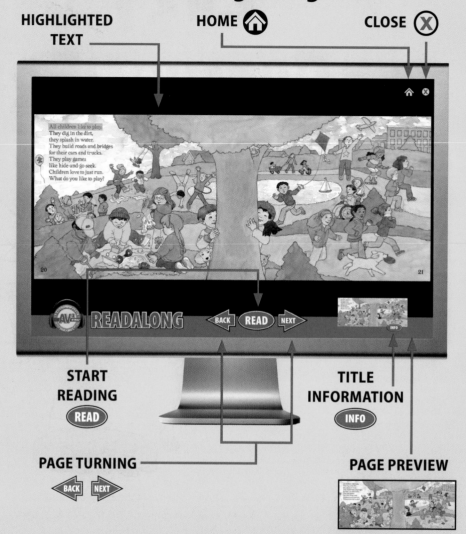

HIGHLIGHTED TEXT

HOME 🏠

CLOSE ⊗

START READING
READ

TITLE INFORMATION
INFO

PAGE TURNING
BACK NEXT

PAGE PREVIEW

Published by AV² by Weigl
350 5ᵗʰ Avenue, 59ᵗʰ Floor New York, NY 10118
Websites: www.av2books.com   www.weigl.com

Library of Congress Control Number: 2014937593

ISBN 978-1-4896-2341-6 (hardcover)
ISBN 978-1-4896-2342-3 (single user eBook)
ISBN 978-1-4896-2343-0 (multi-user eBook)

Printed in the United States of America in North Mankato, Minnesota
1 2 3 4 5 6 7 8 9 0 18 17 16 15 14

042014
WEP250413

Text copyright ©2011 by Mary Ellen Jordan and Andrew Weldon.
Illustrations copyright ©2011 by Andrew Weldon.
Published in 2013 by Albert Whitman & Company.

2

This is my cow,
she's called Daisy.
She should eat grass,
but she's too lazy.

Instead she eats jelly,
spoon after spoon,

all through the morning
till late afternoon.

This is my pig, she's called Nancy.

She should like mud,
but she's too fancy.

Instead she stares
at her reflection,

10

"My oh my,
you are perfection."

11

This is my chicken,
she's called Lizzie.

She should lay eggs,
but she's too busy.

Instead she dances
through the air,

14

in her purple
underwear.

This is my dog, he's called Frankie.

He should chase sheep,
but he's too cranky.

Instead he slumps,
watching TV,

demanding cake
and cups of tea.

This is my farm,
it might not look good.

None of the animals
do what they should.

Except for at night . . .
there's no mooing or barking
or oinking or cheeping.

At least my animals
are good at sleeping.